STELLA
STAR OF THE SEA

MARIE-LOUISE GAY

A GROUNDWOOD BOOK   DOUGLAS & McINTYRE   TORONTO VANCOUVER BUFFALO

Groundwood Books / Douglas & McIntyre Ltd.
720 Bathurst Street, Suite 500, Toronto, Ontario M5S 2R4

Distributed in the U.S.A. by Publishers Group West
1700 Fourth Street, Berkeley, CA 94710

We acknowledge the financial support of the Canada Council for the Arts, the Ontario
Arts Council and the Government of Canada through the Book Publishing Industry
Development Program for our publishing activities.

Canadian Cataloguing in Publication Data
Gay, Marie-Louise
Stella, star of the sea
A Groundwood book.
ISBN 0-88899-395-1
I. Title.
PS8563.A868S73 1999   jC813'.54   C98-932383-8
PZ7.G39St 1999

Printed and bound in China by Everbest Printing Co. Ltd.

To Jacob, who always wants to know why

Stella and Sam were spending a day at the seashore.
It was Sam's very first time.

"Isn't it beautiful, Sam?" asked Stella.
"It's very big," said Sam, "and noisy."

Stella had seen the sea once, before Sam was born.
She knew all its secrets.

"Is the water cold?" asked Sam. "Is it deep?
Are there any sea monsters?"

"The water is lovely," said Stella.
"And not a sea monster in sight.
Come on in, Sam!"

"Not right now," said Sam.

"Where do starfish come from?" asked Sam.
"From the sky," answered Stella.

"Starfish are shooting stars
that fell in love with the sea."

"Weren't the stars afraid of drowning?" asked Sam.

"No," said Stella. "They all learned how to swim."

"What is this?" asked Sam.
"It's a moon shell," said Stella. "It comes from the moon."
"What is that?" asked Sam.

"It's an angel wing," said Stella. "It comes from an angel."
"And this?" asked Sam.
"It's a shark's eye," said Stella.

"Do you think there are sharks in the sea?" asked Sam.
"Have you ever seen one?"

"Just a little one," said Stella, "with an eyepatch.
Are you coming, Sam?"
"Not just this minute," said Sam.

"Come see, Sam," called Stella. "I found a sea horse."

"Does a sea horse neigh?" asked Sam.
"Does a sea horse gallop?"

"Yes!" cried Stella. "And you can ride a sea horse bareback.
Come on in, Sam!"

"Not right now," said Sam.

"Let's dig a very deep hole," said Stella.

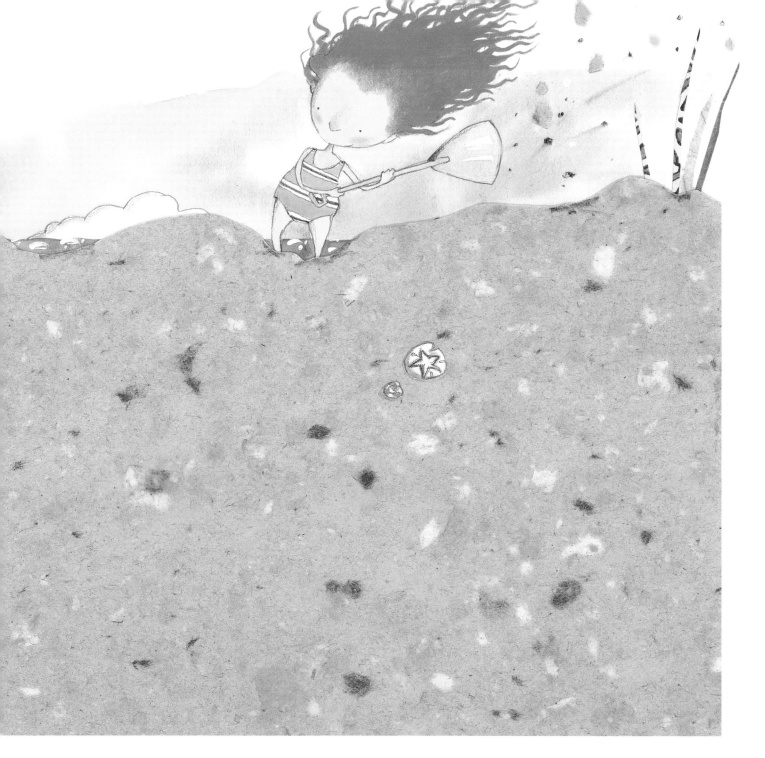

"Why?" asked Sam. "What for?
Where will we end up?"

"In China," answered Stella.
"Are we there yet?" asked Sam.

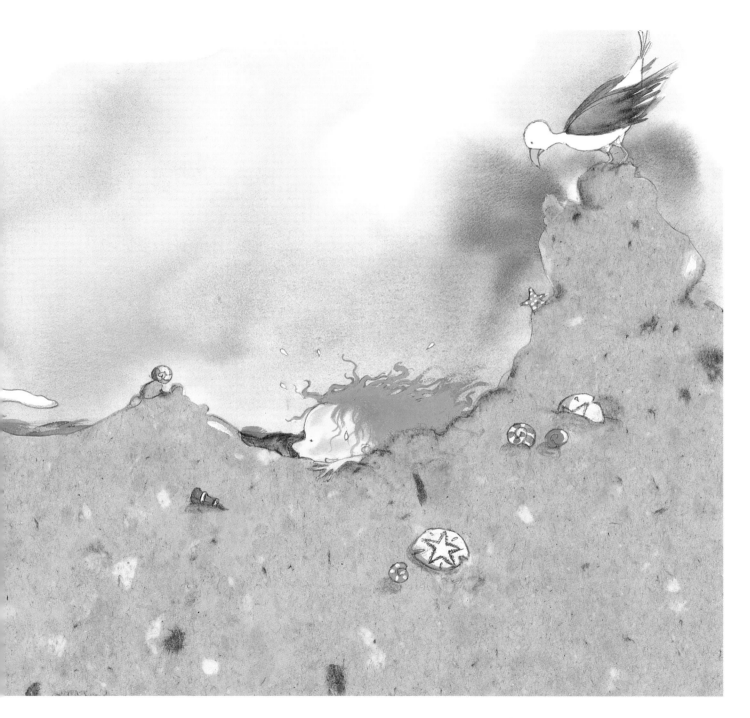

"Let's go fishing, Sam," sighed Stella.
"Maybe we'll catch a catfish."

"Does a catfish purr?" asked Sam.
"Does a dogfish bark?
Does a toadfish croak?" asked Sam.

"I don't know," sighed Stella. "I'm going swimming."
"Does a parrotfish swim?" asked Sam.
"Or does it fly and squawk?"

"Does the sea touch the sky?" asked Sam.
"Do boats sail off the edge?
Where do waves come from? Why..."

"Sam!!" yelled Stella. "Are you ever coming in?"

"YES!" said Sam.